Dear Parent:
Your child's love of reading

Every child learns to read in a different way and at his or her own speed. Some go back and forth between reading levels and read favorite books again and again. Others read through each level in order. You can help your young reader improve and become more confident by encouraging his or her own interests and abilities. From books your child reads with you to the first books he or she reads alone, there are I Can Read Books for every stage of reading:

SHARED READING
Basic language, word repetition, and whimsical illustrations, ideal for sharing with your emergent reader

BEGINNING READING
Short sentences, familiar words, and simple concepts for children eager to read on their own

READING WITH HELP
Engaging stories, longer sentences, and language play for developing readers

READING ALONE
Complex plots, challenging vocabulary, and high-interest topics for the independent reader

ADVANCED READING
Short paragraphs, chapters, and exciting themes for the perfect bridge to chapter books

I Can Read Books have introduced children to the joy of reading since 1957. Featuring award-winning authors and illustrators and a fabulous cast of beloved characters, I Can Read Books set the standard for beginning readers.

A lifetime of discovery begins with the magical words "I Can Read!"

Visit www.icanread.com for information
on enriching your child's reading experience.

I Can Read® is a trademark of HarperCollins Publishers.

Batman: Dawn of the Dynamic Duo
Copyright © 2011 DC Comics.
BATMAN and all related characters and elements are trademarks of and © DC Comics.
(s11)

DCHARP2513

Manufactured in China. No part of this book may be used or reproduced in any manner whatsoever without written permission except in the case of brief quotations embodied in critical articles and reviews. For information address HarperCollins Children's Books, a division of HarperCollins Publishers, 195 Broadway, New York, NY 10007.
www.icanread.com

Library of congress Catalog card number: 2011924604
ISBN 978-0-06-188520-4
Book design by John Sazaklis

15 16 17 18 19 20   SCP   10 9   ❖   First Edition

I Can Read! Reading 2 With Help

BATMAN™

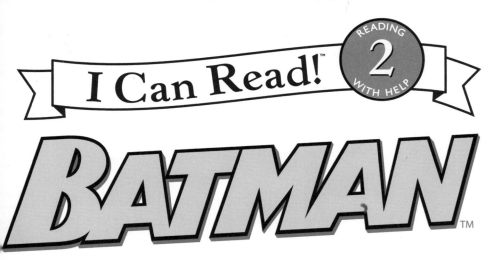

Dawn of the Dynamic Duo

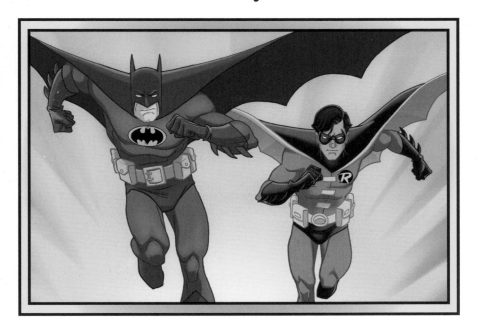

by John Sazaklis

pictures by Steven E. Gordon

colors by Eric A. Gordon

BATMAN created by Bob Kane

HARPER

An Imprint of HarperCollins*Publishers*

BRUCE WAYNE

Bruce is a rich businessman. Orphaned as a child, he trained his body and mind to become Batman, the Caped Crusader.

TIM DRAKE

Tim is in high school. He is smart and athletic. He is also Robin.

TWO-FACE

Former district attorney Harvey Dent lost his mind when half his face was scarred by acid. Now two men trapped in one body, he bases his crimes on the flip of his special coin.

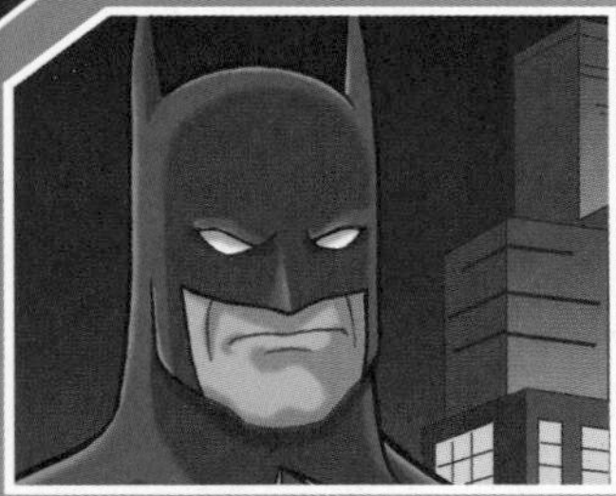

BATMAN

Batman is an expert martial artist, crime fighter, and inventor. He is known as the World's Greatest Detective.

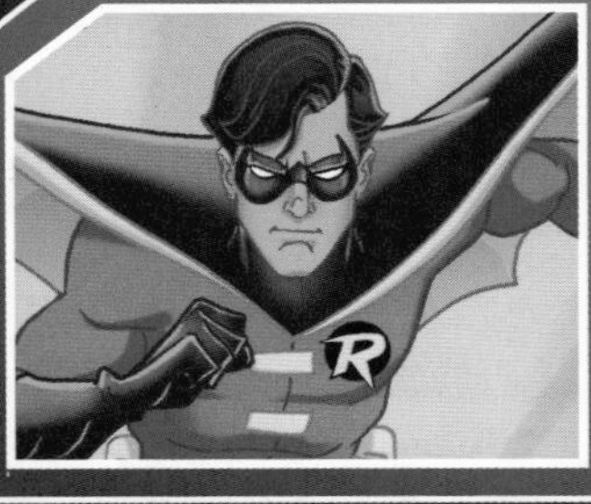
R

ROBIN

Robin is Batman's partner and sidekick. Together they keep Gotham City safe. Robin is also known as the Boy Wonder.

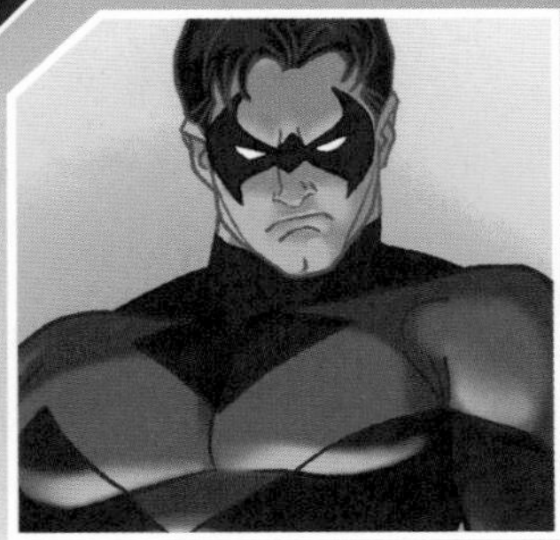

NIGHTWING

The original Robin, Dick Grayson grew up and became the hero Nightwing. He protects a city near Gotham and sometimes helps Batman.

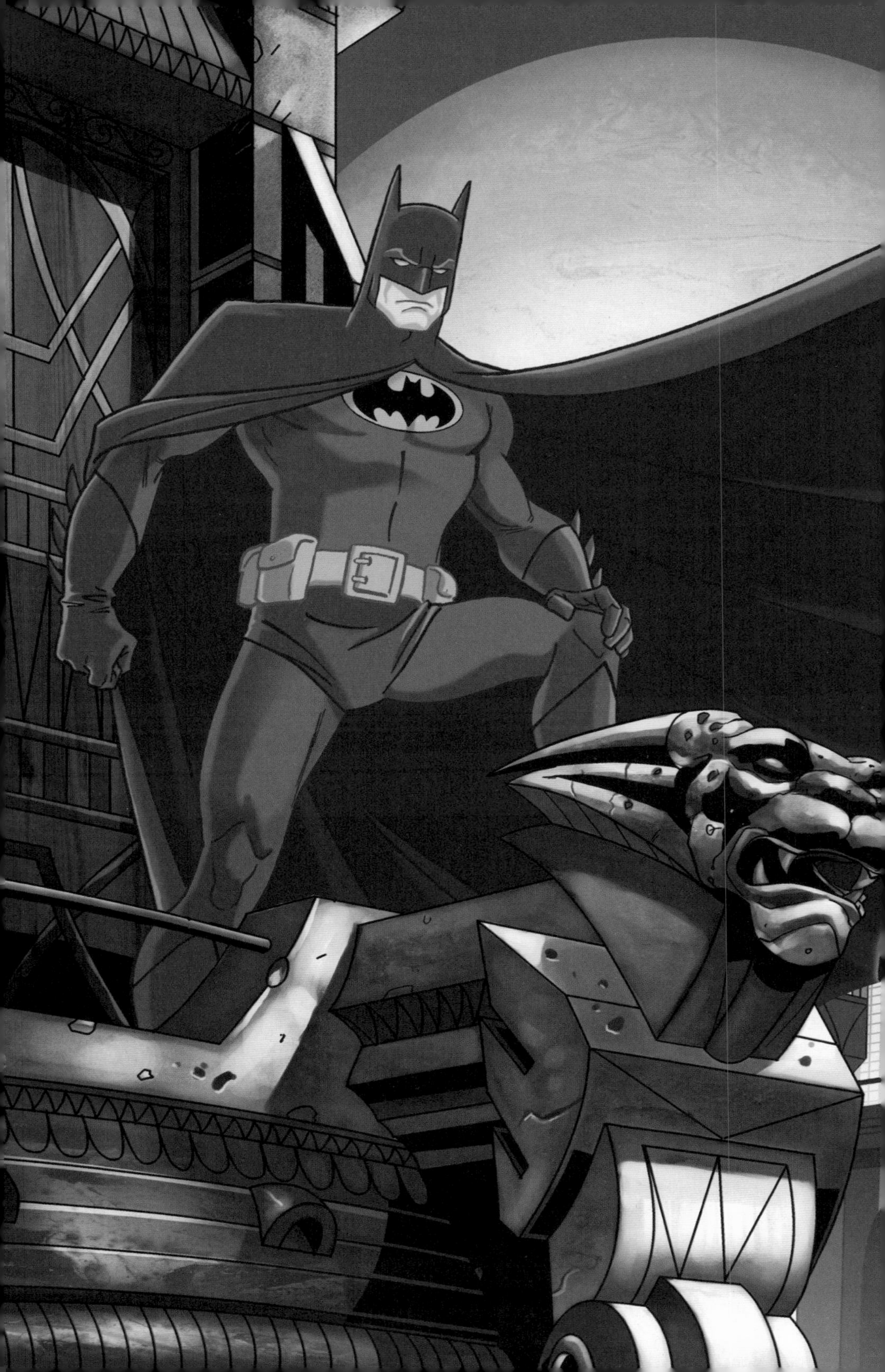

Gotham City is a dark
and scary place.
One man helps the police
protect the innocent.
He is a silent guardian.
He is Batman.

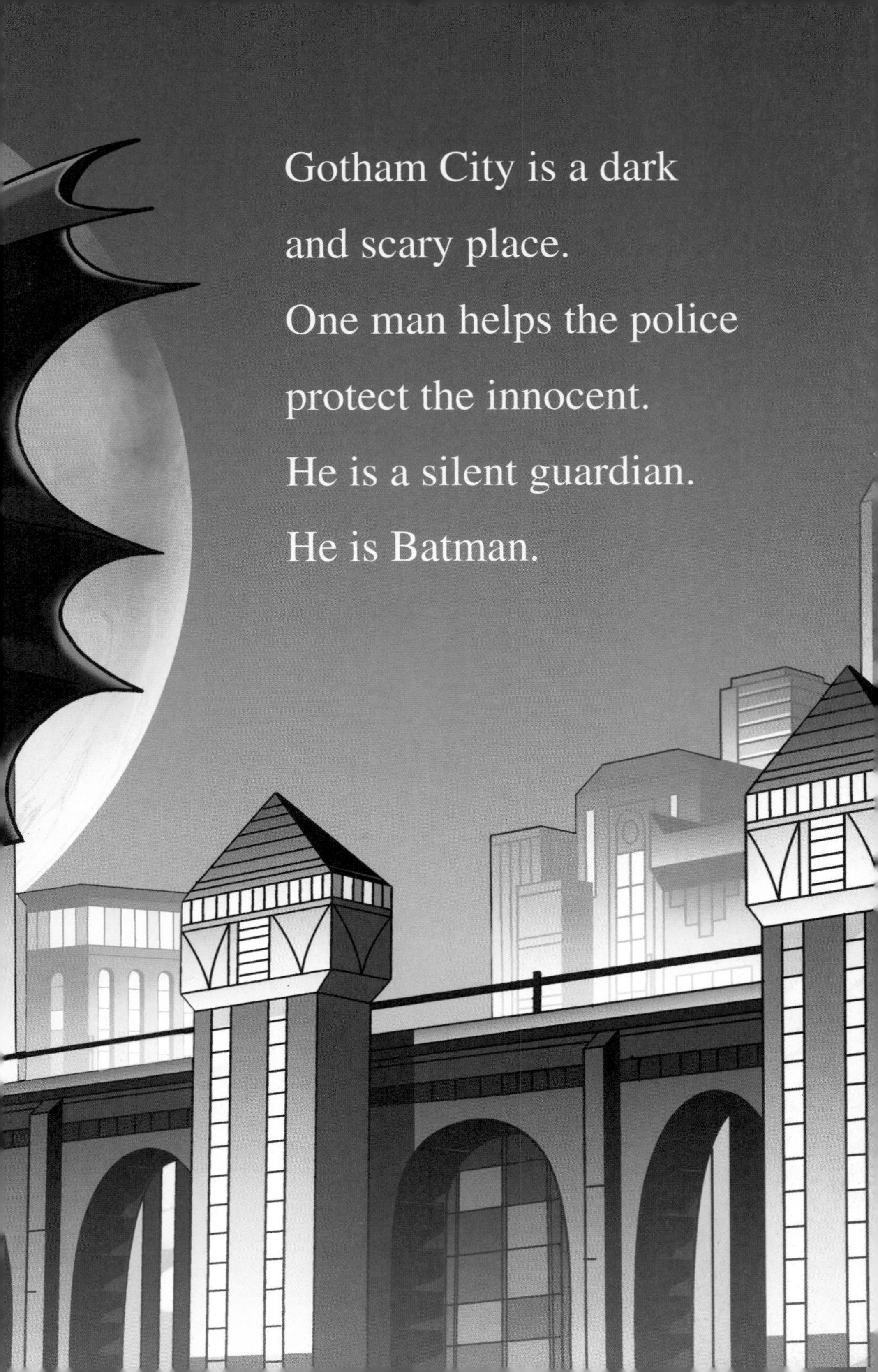

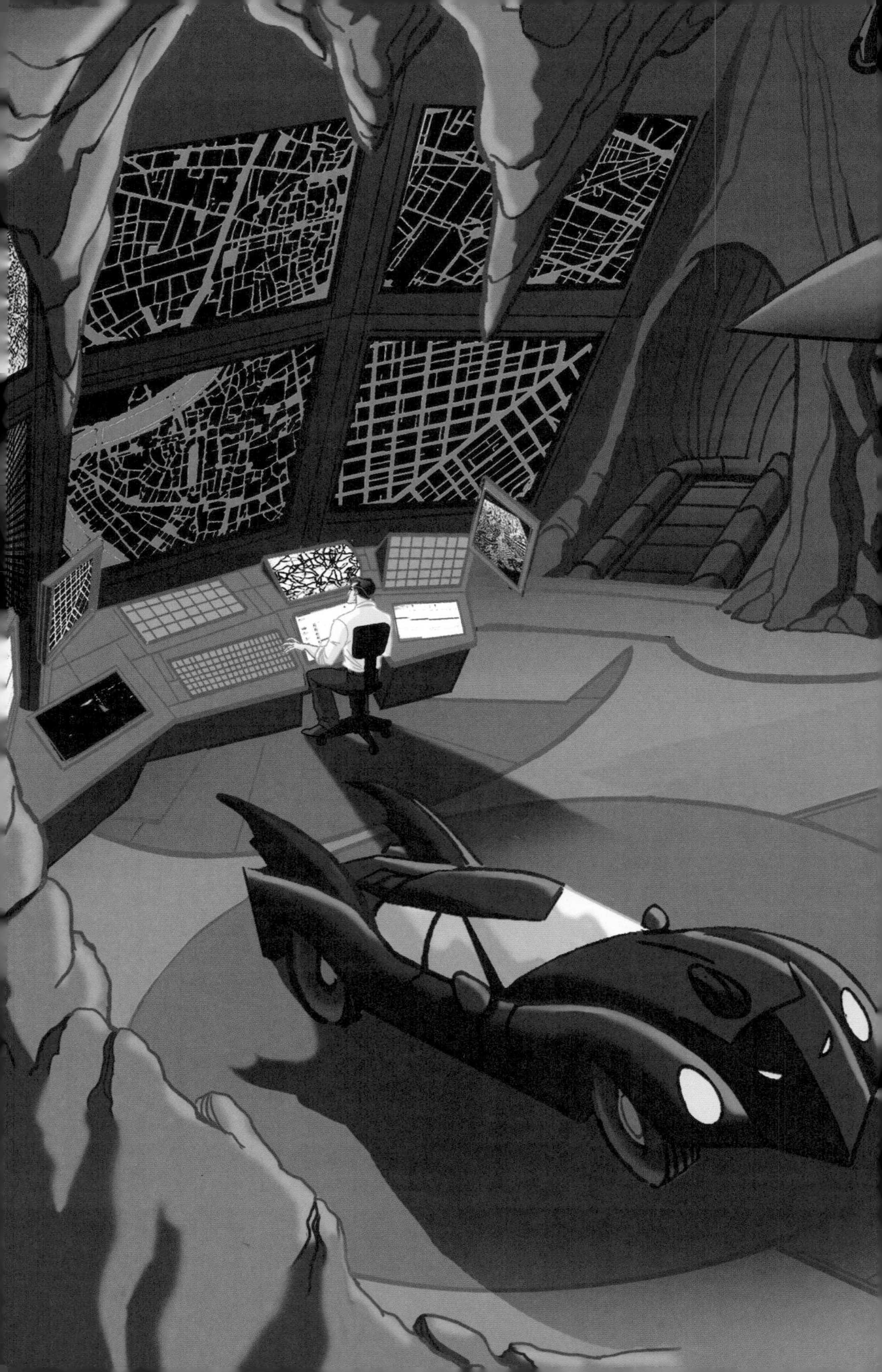

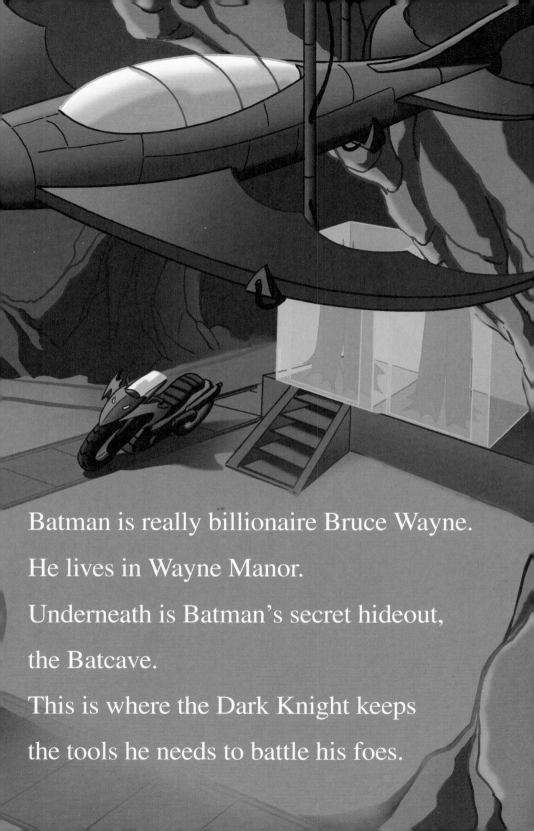

Batman is really billionaire Bruce Wayne.

He lives in Wayne Manor.

Underneath is Batman's secret hideout,
the Batcave.

This is where the Dark Knight keeps
the tools he needs to battle his foes.

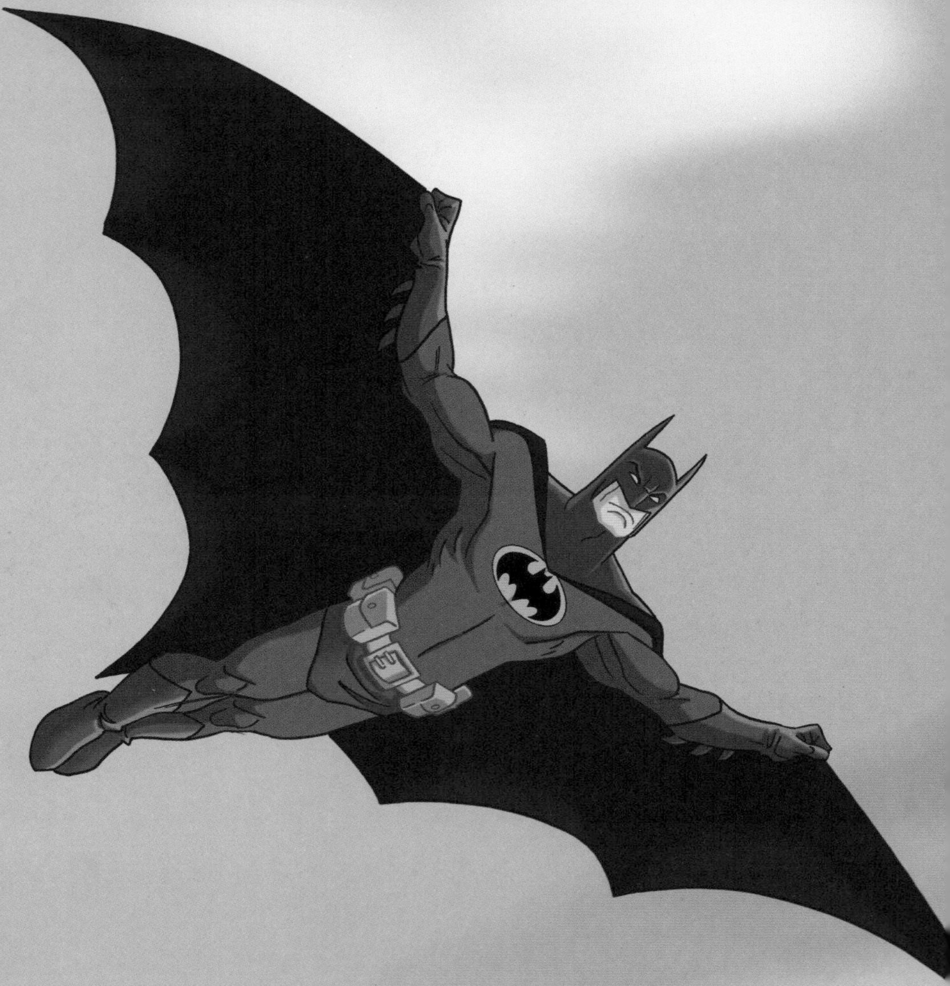

Batman cannot protect the city alone.
He has a sidekick named Robin.
Robin is a skilled crime fighter
and junior detective.

Together, Batman and Robin are the Dynamic Duo!

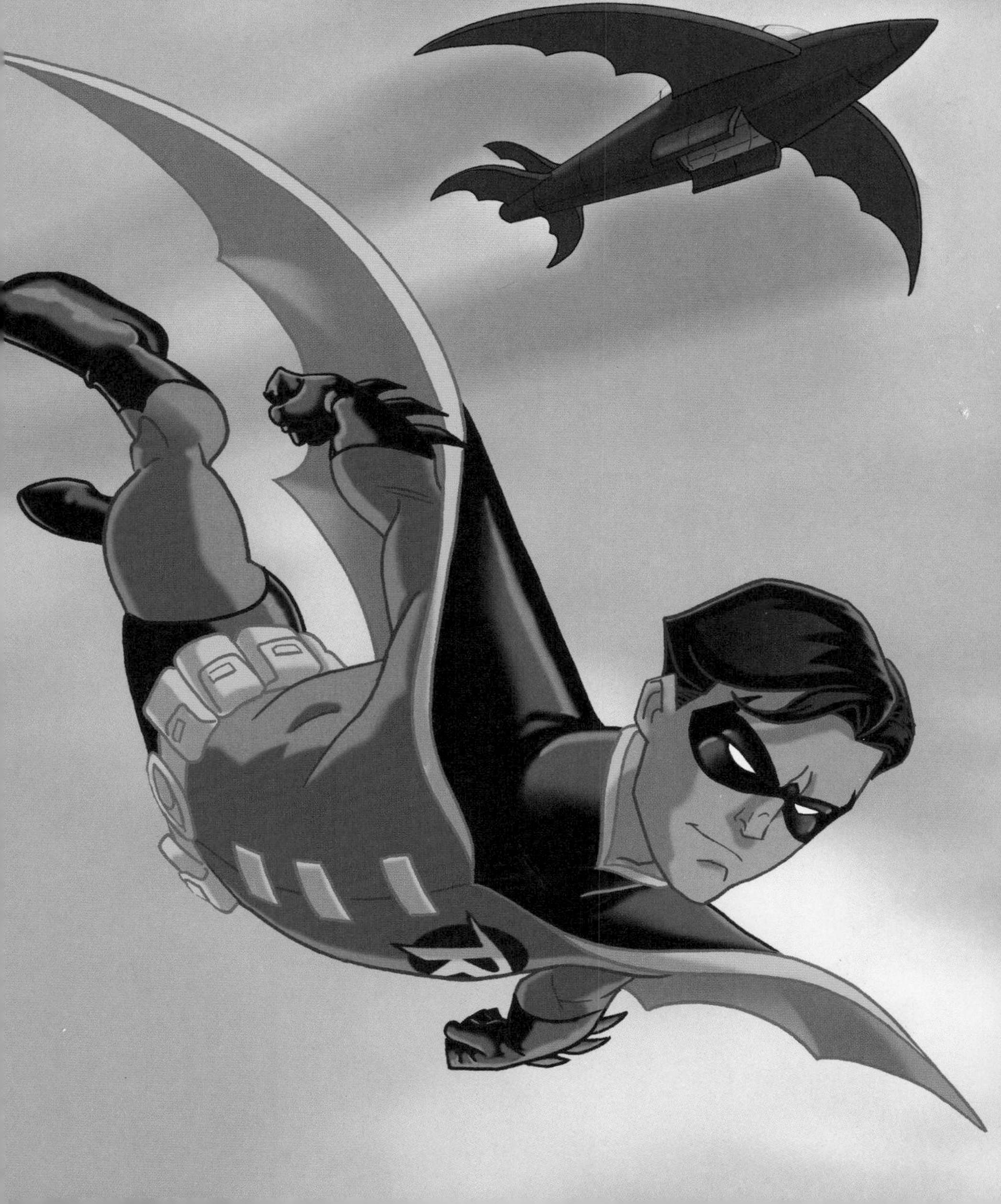

Robin’s real name is Tim Drake.
Tim is a straight-A student
and a star athlete.

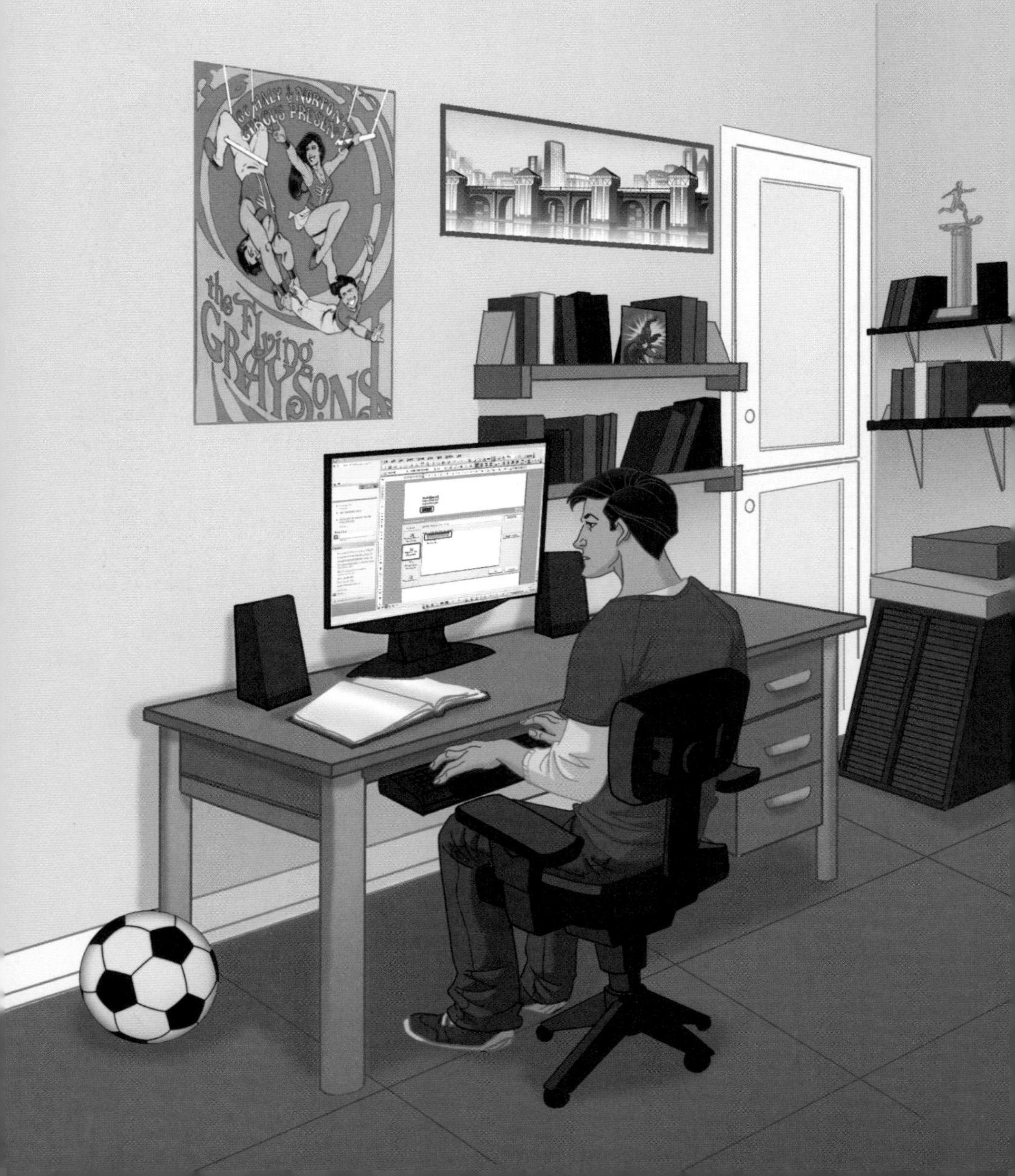
the Flying
GRAYSONS

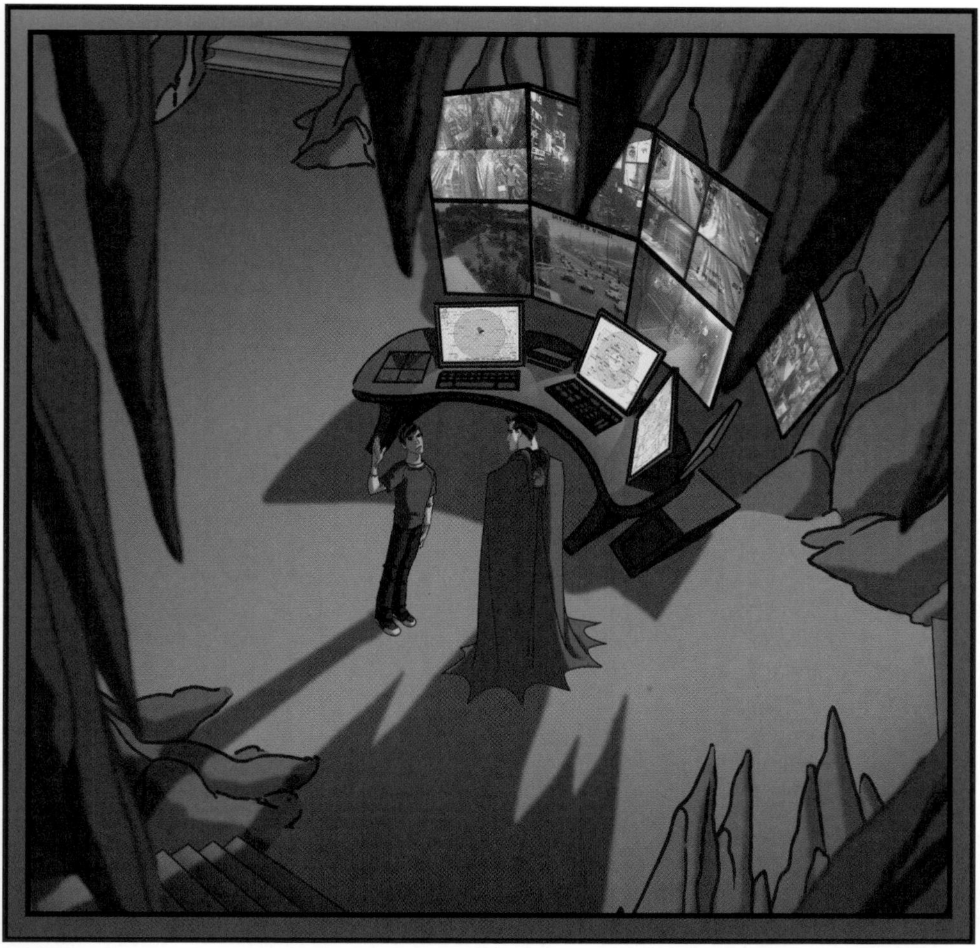

Before he became Robin,
Tim took an oath
to be Batman's partner
and to keep his secret safe.

Tim trained for many months.

He had the best teacher in the world . . .

Batman himself!

Tim learned martial arts, gymnastics,

and how to use different weapons.

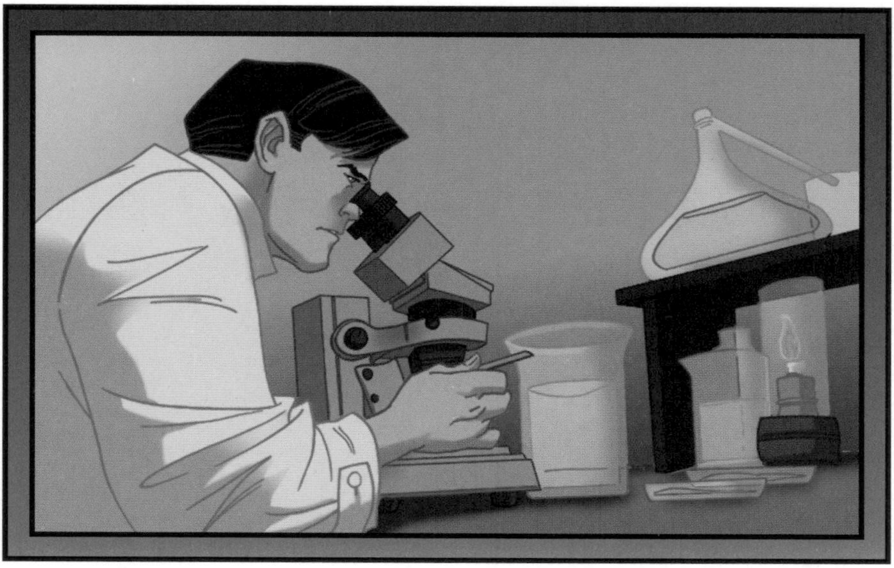

He also used science to solve crimes.

When Tim was finally ready,

Batman gave Tim his Robin suit.

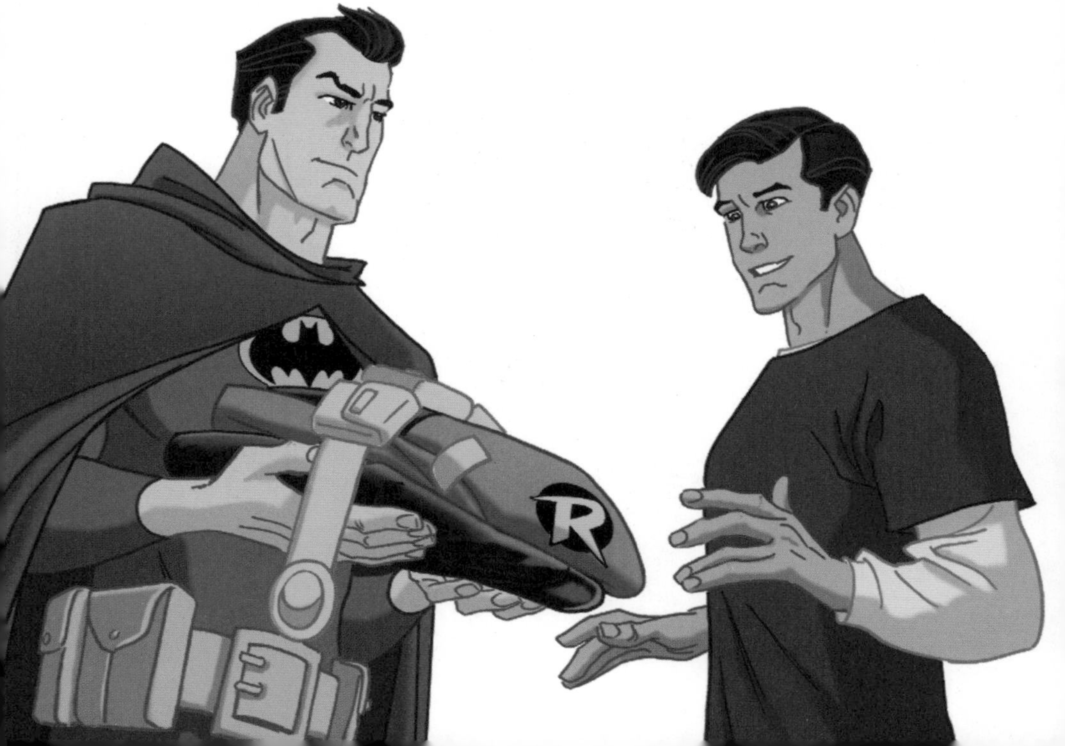

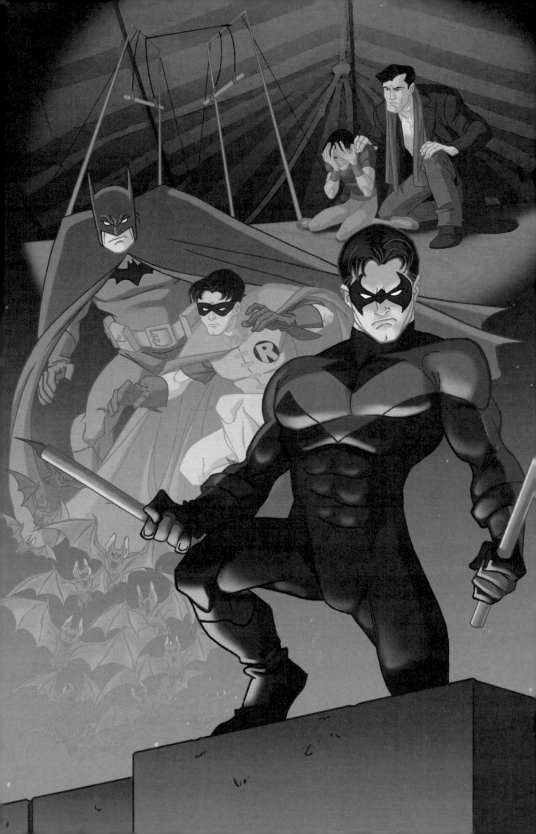

Tim Drake is not the first Robin.

Batman's original sidekick

was a boy named Dick Grayson.

Dick, an orphaned acrobat,

was adopted by Bruce Wayne.

He was also trained to fight crime

as Robin, the Boy Wonder.

When Dick grew older,

he became the hero Nightwing.

Sometimes, he still helps Batman

protect Gotham City.

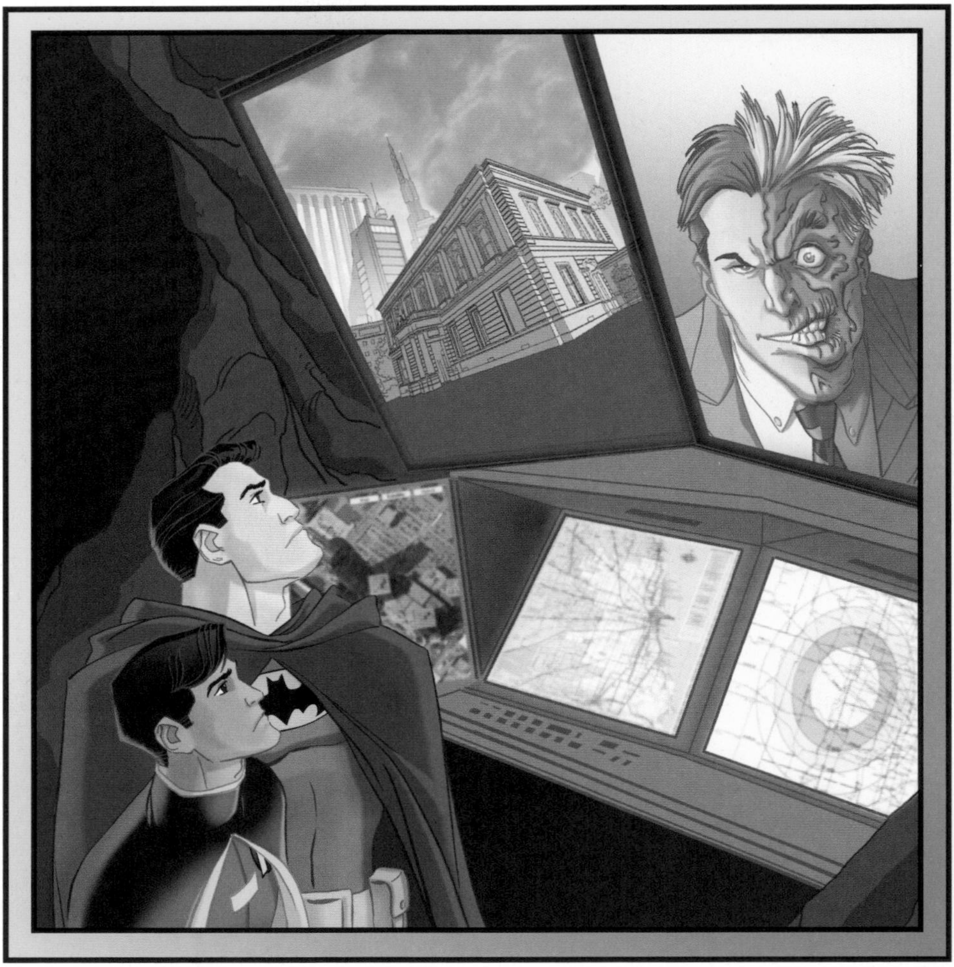

Bruce and Tim are in the Batcave
when an alarm blares.
There's trouble at the Gotham City Mint.
"It's Two-Face!" Tim yells.

Batman and Robin suit up.

"To the Batmobile!" Batman says.

The heroes zoom into action.

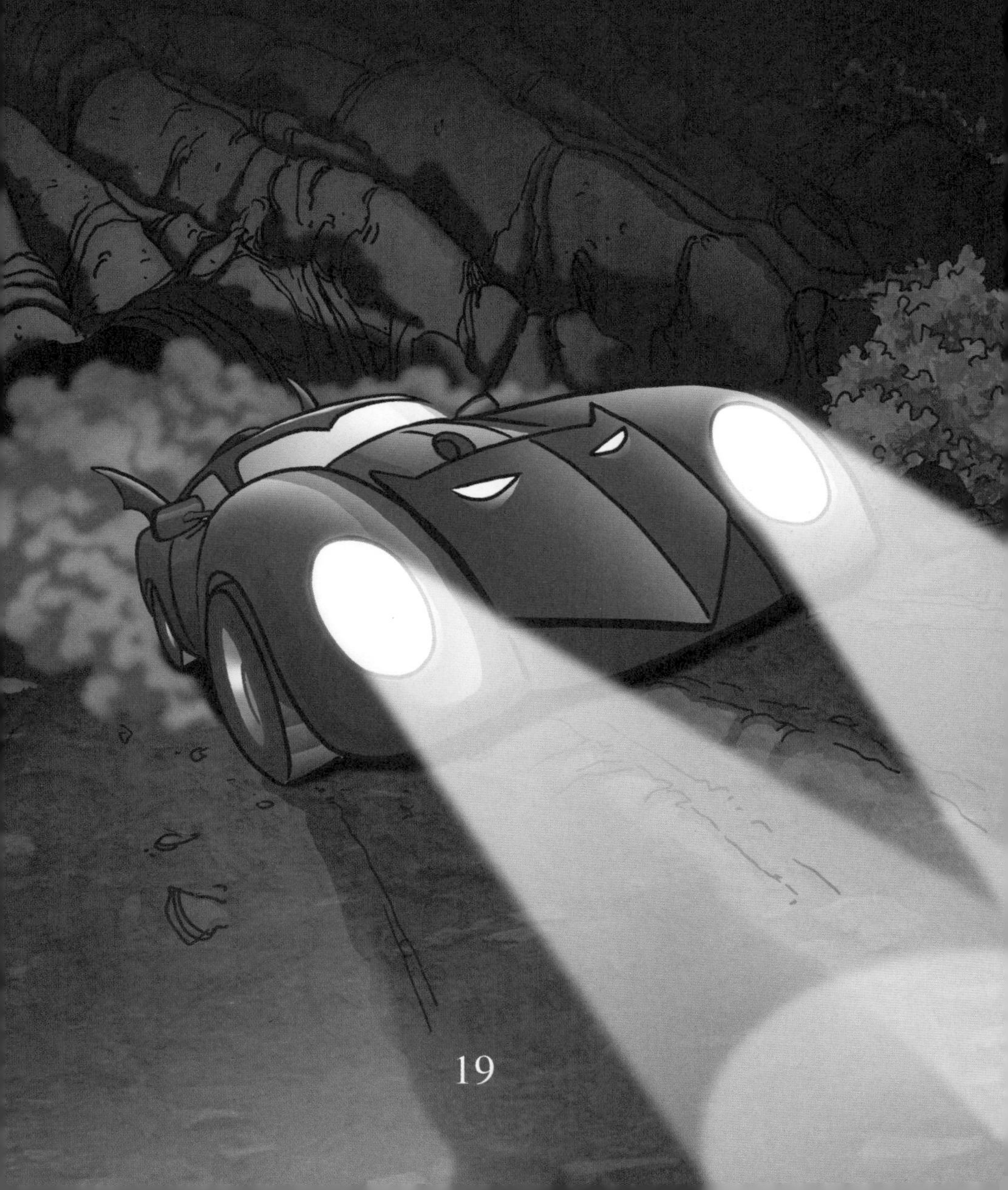

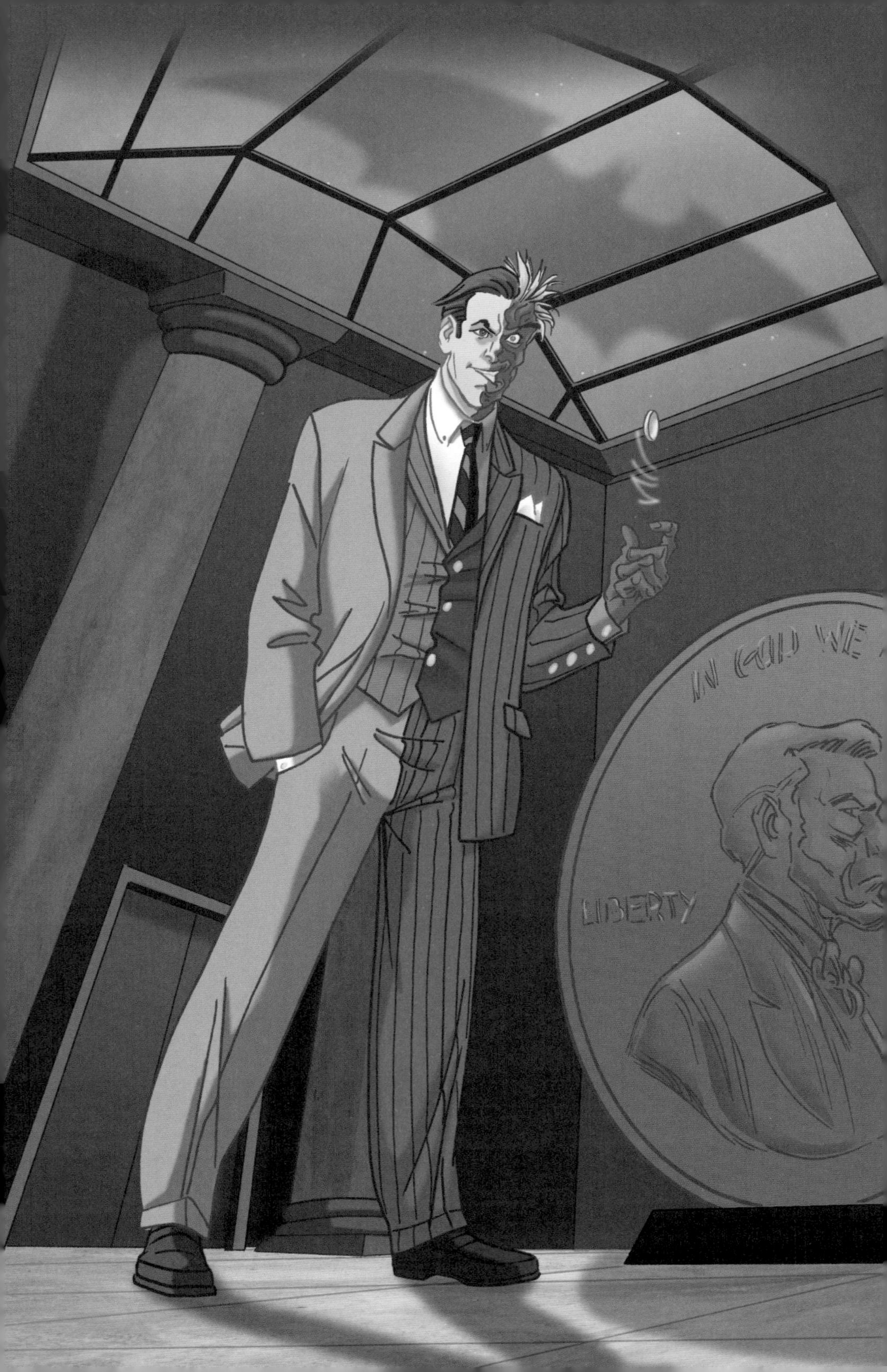
IN GOD WE
LIBERTY

At the mint, Two-Face flips his coin.

"Heads, we steal HALF the cash.

Tails, we steal ALL the cash!"

the crook cackles.

His henchmen are known

as the Two-Ton Gang.

They break into the vault.

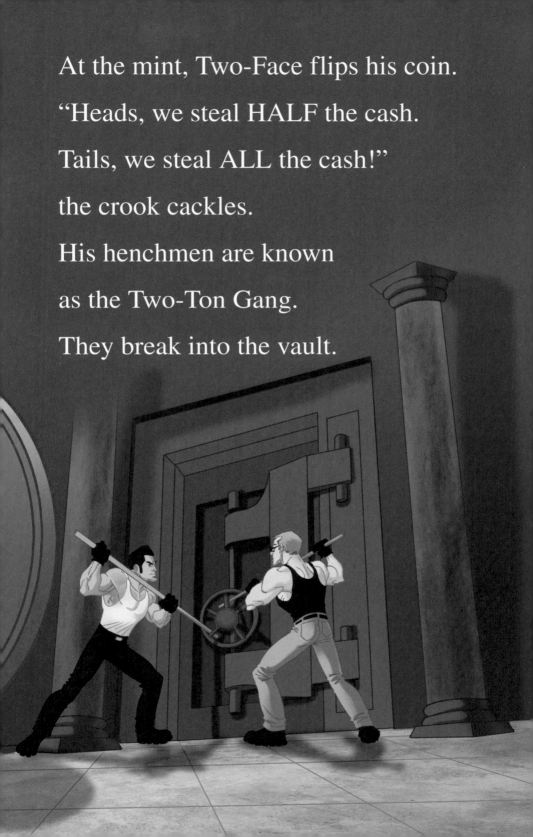

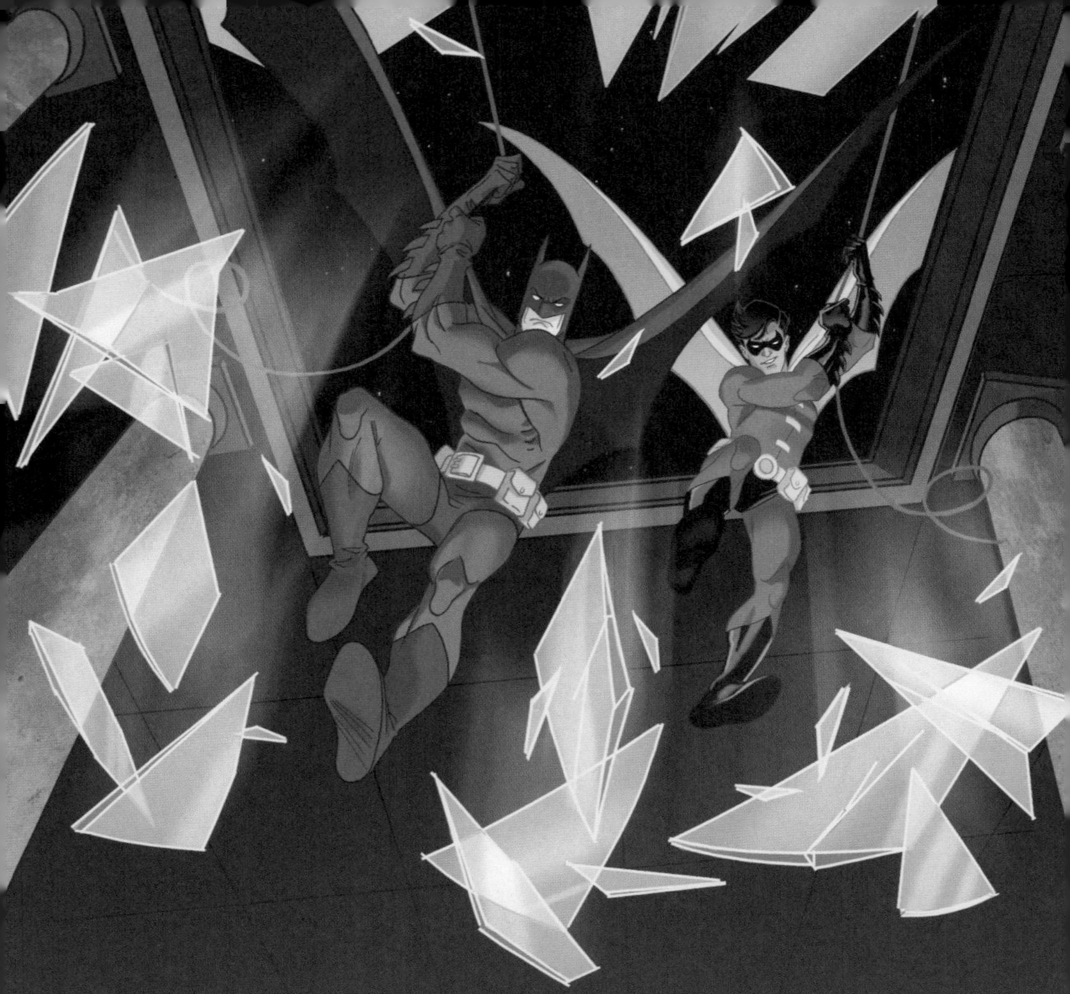

As Two-Face reaches for his riches
the Dynamic Duo bursts in.
"Drop the dough!" says Robin.
"Heads up, boys," Two-Face cries.
"It's the bat and the brat!"

After a long fight,
the heroes are overpowered
by the superstrong goons.
"Looks like you're in double trouble,"
Two-Face says to the duo.

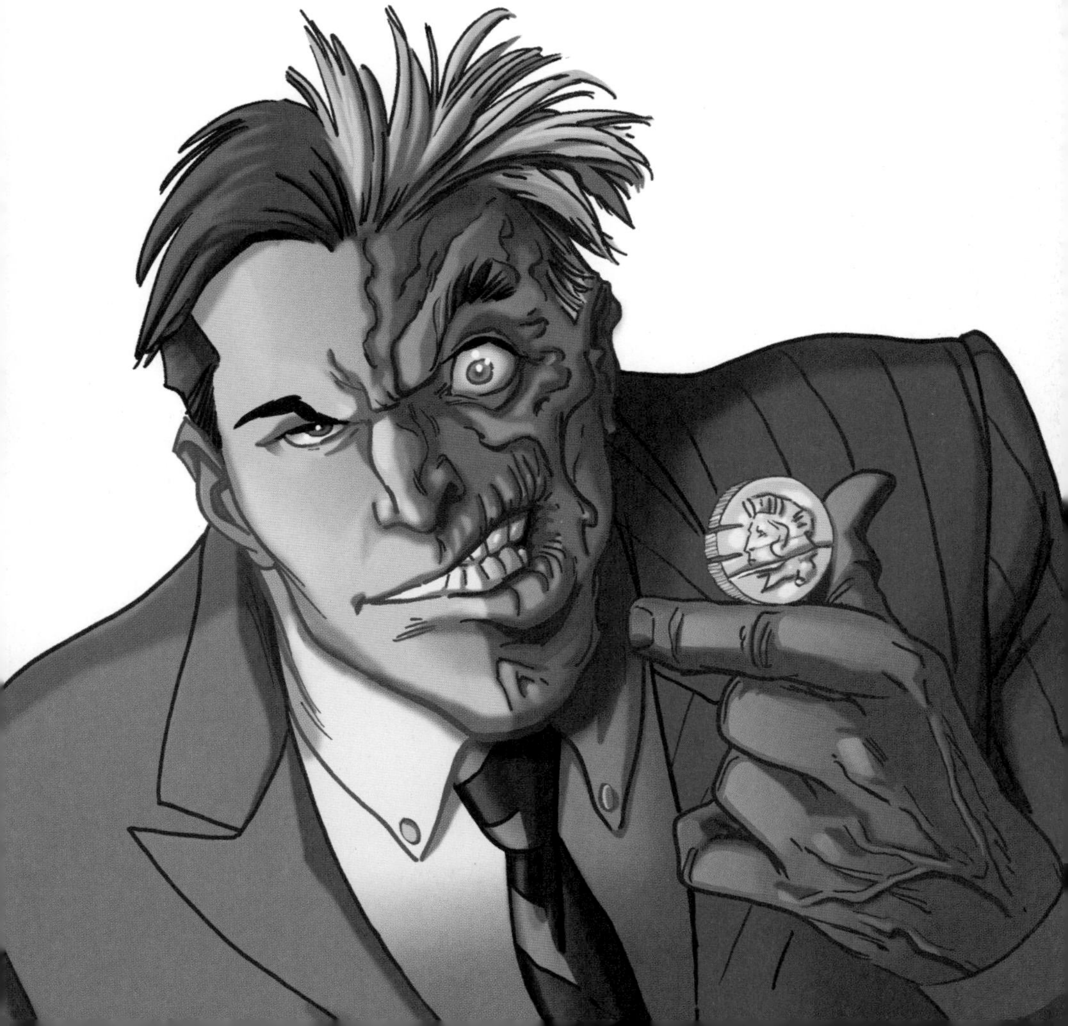

The Two-Ton Gang ties up

Batman and Robin.

Each hero is strapped to one side of the

giant penny in the display.

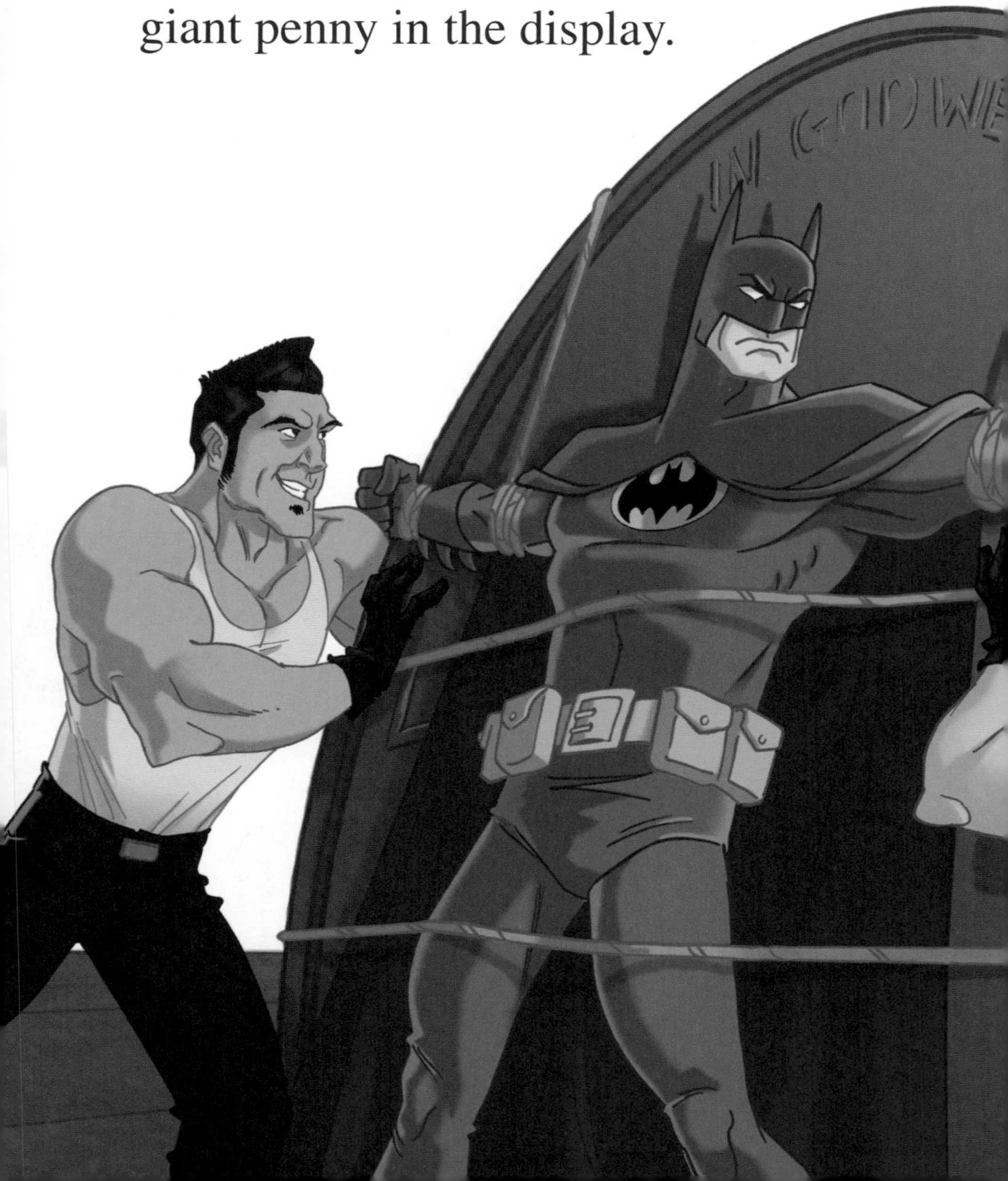

Two-Face has an evil plan.
"Let's break up the set,"
the villain snarls.
"Flip the coin and flatten a foe!"

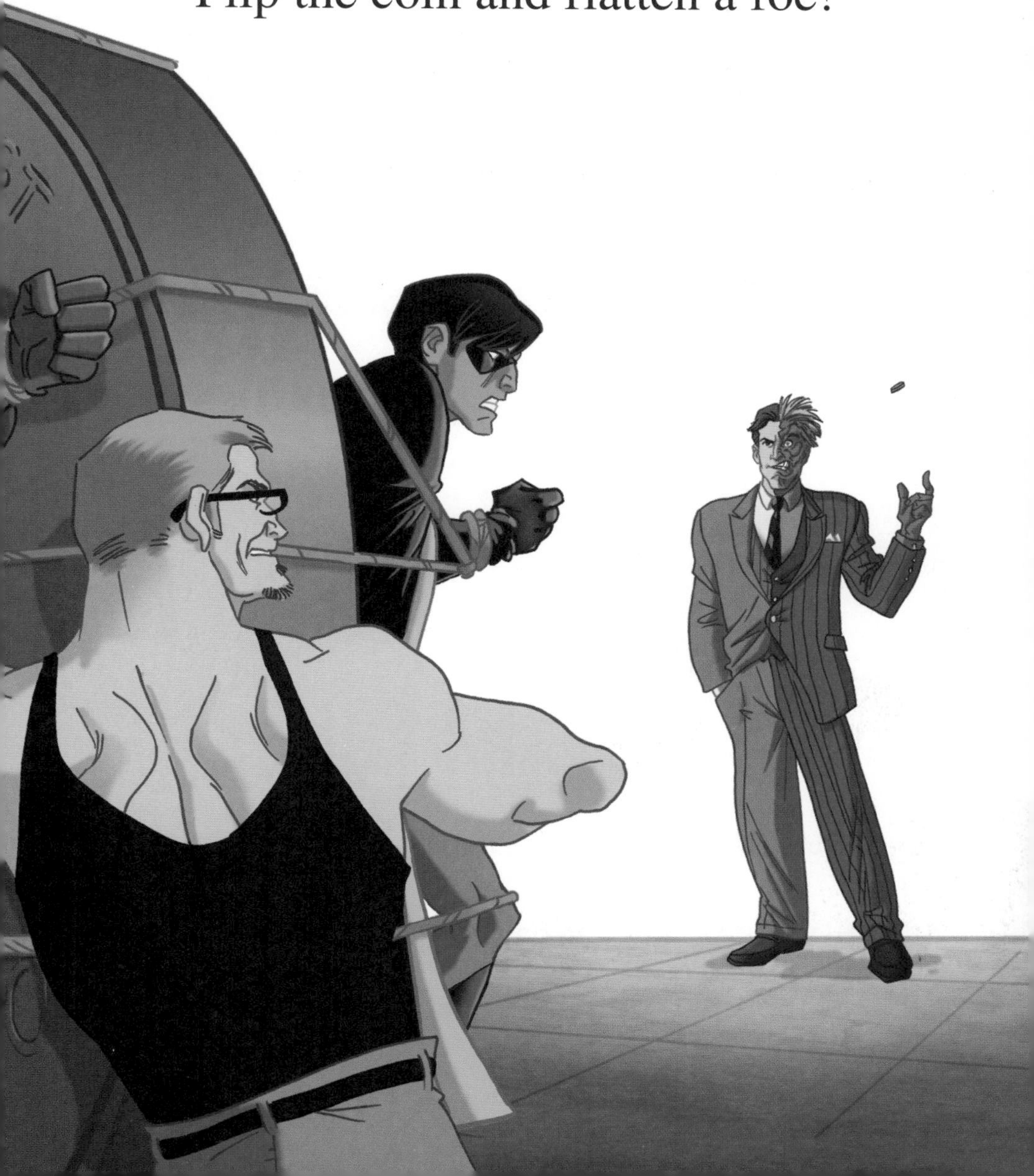

"Don't be so smug," Batman replies.

"This isn't over yet."

Suddenly, a smoke bomb explodes

and blinds the robbers.

When the smoke clears,

Batman and Robin are free,

and they have a friend by their side.

“Nightwing!” Two-Face cries.

“It’s a triple threat!” says Nightwing.

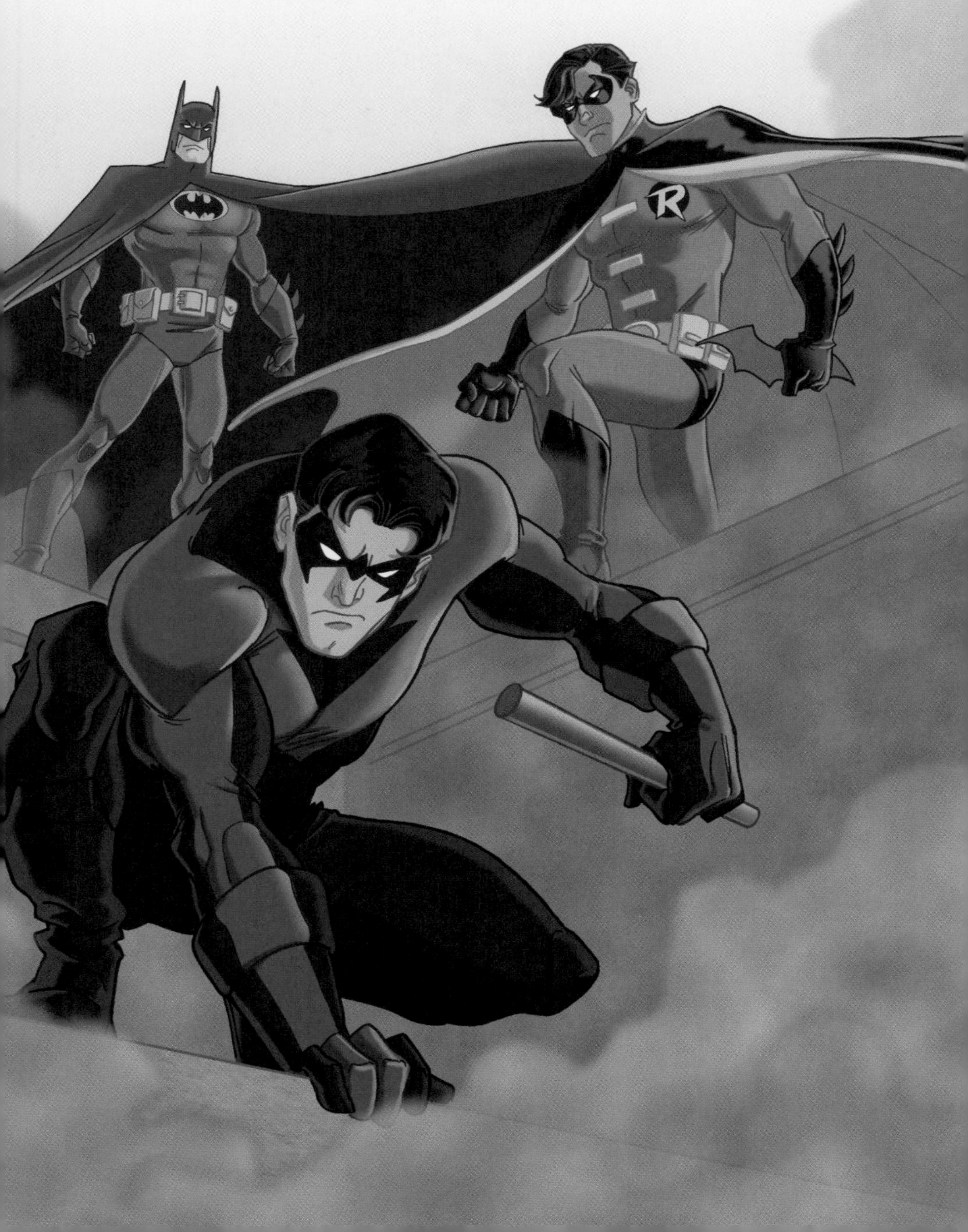

“Get them, you fools!” yells Two-Face.

The Two-Ton Gang rushes at the heroes.

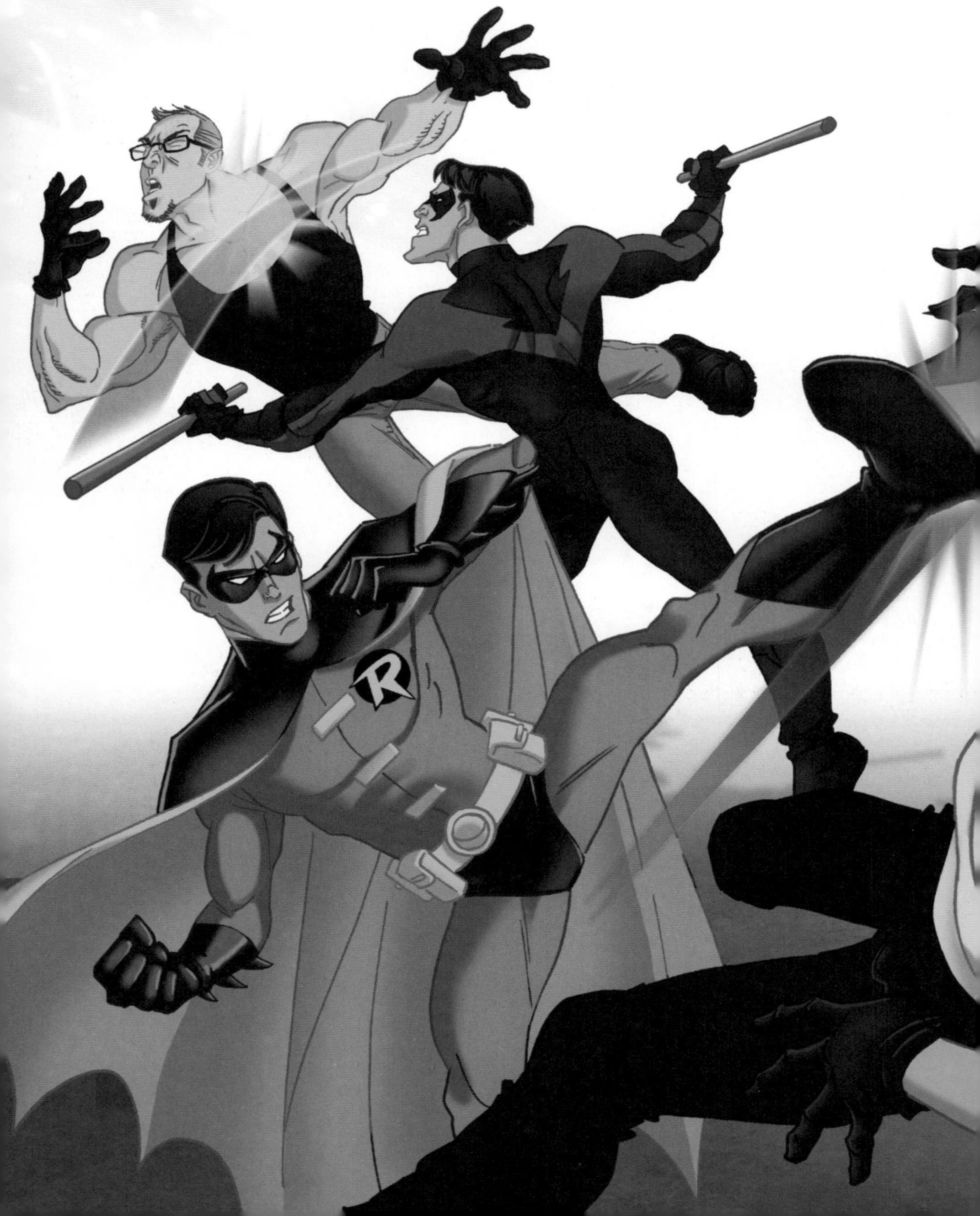

Nightwing helps even out the odds.
He and Robin take on the thugs
as Batman tackles Two-Face.
After a brief battle,
the heroes save the day.

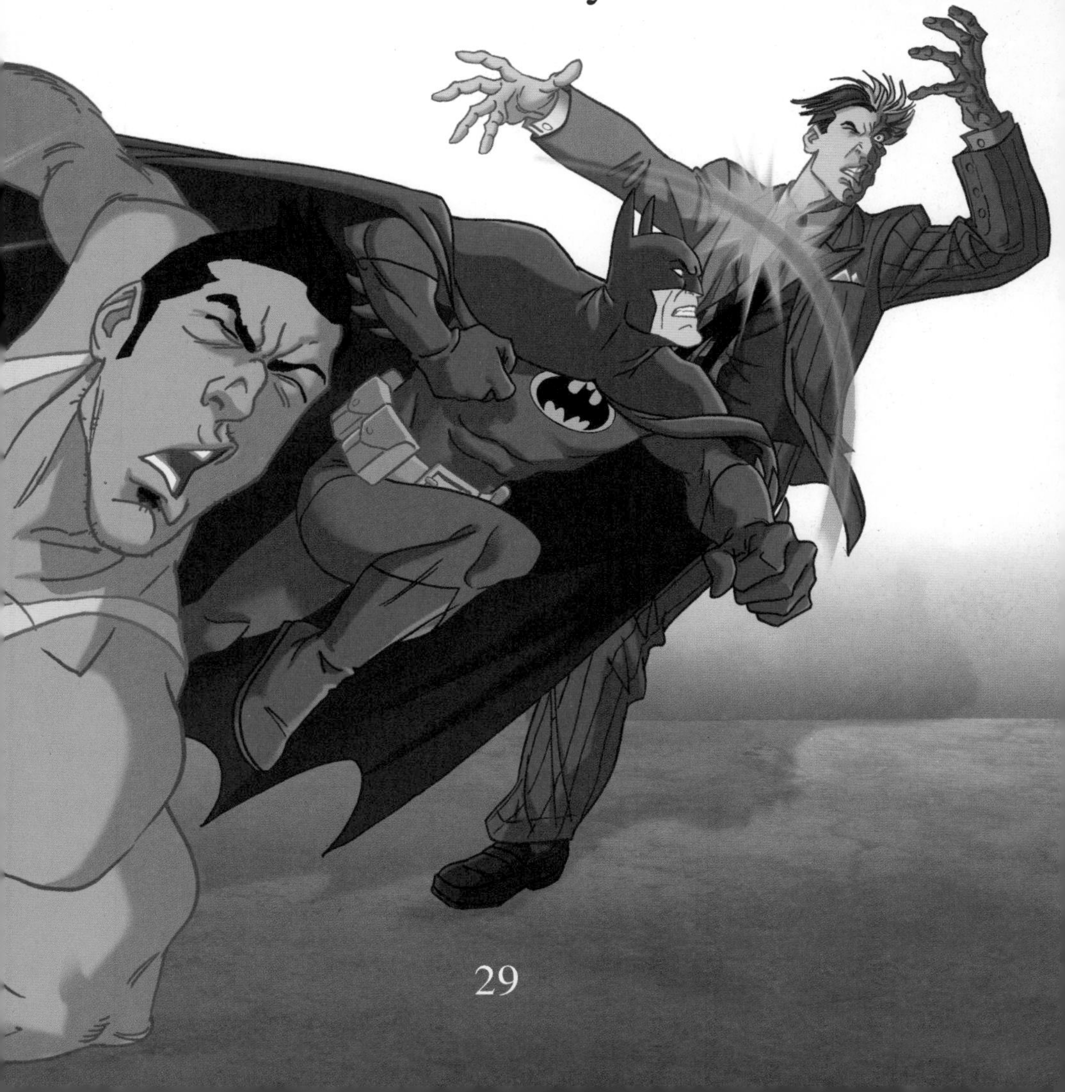

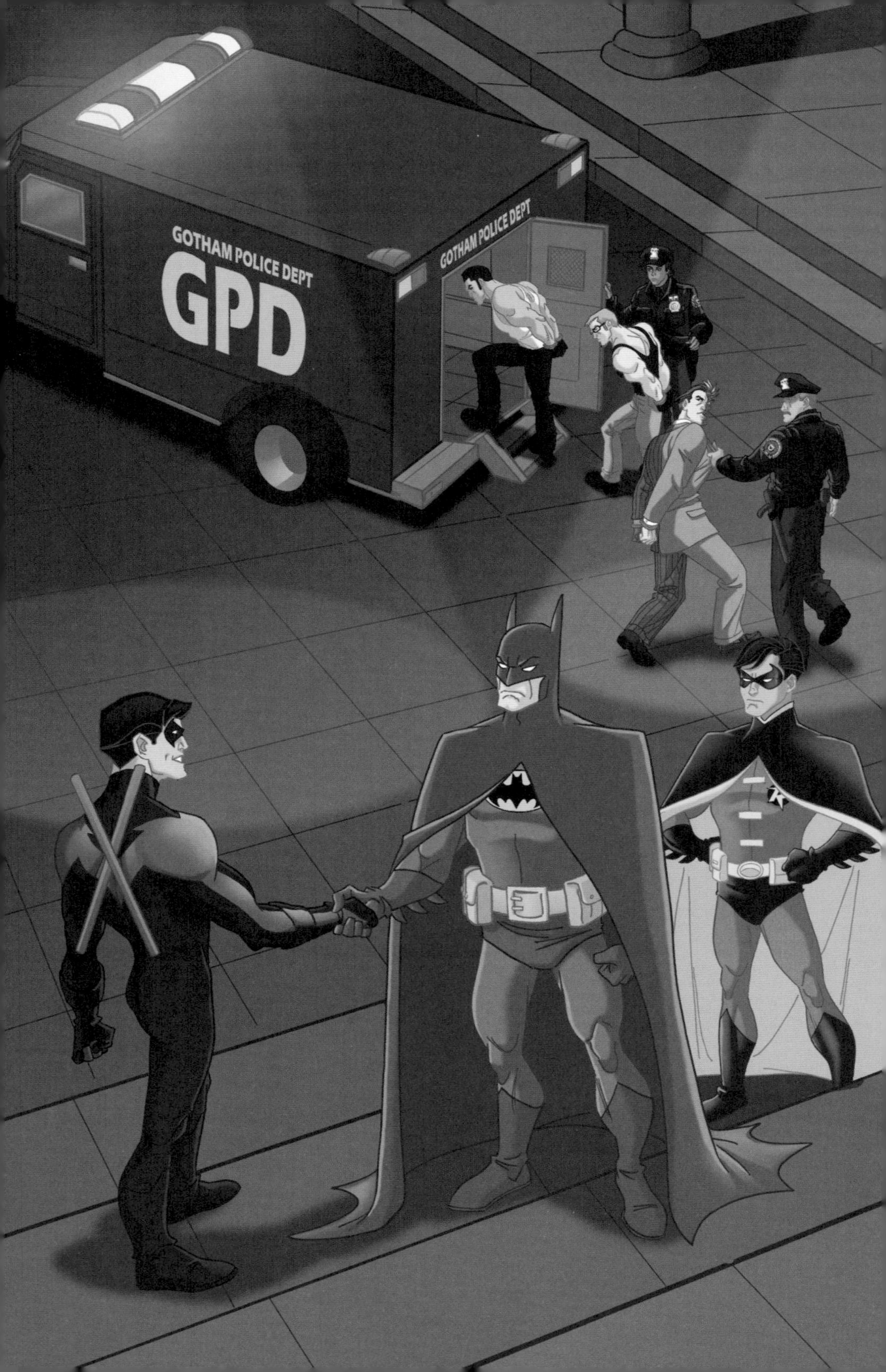
GOTHAM POLICE DEPT
GPD
GOTHAM POLICE DEPT

While the police take the crooks to jail,

Batman thanks Nightwing for his help.

"You're lucky I was in the area,"

Nightwing replies with a smile.

"I'm always glad to lend a hand."

Then Nightwing turns to Robin.

"Batman has taught you well.

You two are truly a Dynamic Duo."

Then the visiting hero

disappears into the night.

"We can't rely on luck," Batman says.
"We must keep training to stay smarter,
stronger, and faster than our foes."
"You're right, Batman," says Robin.
"Back to the Batcave!"

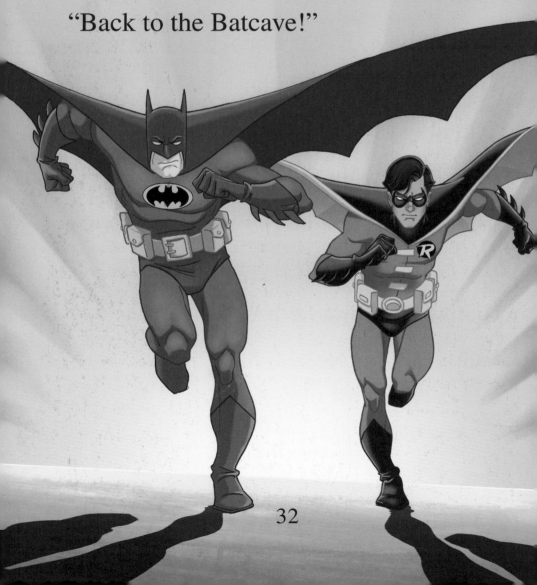